WILT

Ghost

Prepare to be frightened by these terrifying tales from around Wiltshire

By

Richard Holland

BRADWELL
BOOKS

Published by Bradwell Books
9 Orgreave Close Sheffield S13 9NP
Email: books@bradwellbooks.co.uk

British Library Cataloguing in Publication Data: a catalogue
record for this book is available from
the British Library.

1st Edition

ISBN: 9781909914964

Print: Gomer Press, Llandysul, Ceredigion SA44 4JL

Design and Typesetting by: jenksdesign@yahoo.co.uk

Photograph Credits: iStock and R. Holland

CONTENTS

*Salisbury Cathedral is one of Wiltshire's more
spectacular haunted locations.*
iStock

A remarkable apparition was witnessed on the wooded crown of Cherhill Down
©Richard Holland

INTRODUCTION

Wiltshire is a large, mainly rural, county in southern England. Dramatic downs overlook rolling fields and plains peppered with picturesque villages and historic market towns. More than half of Wiltshire's open spaces are categorized as Areas of Outstanding Natural Beauty. Its towns, including Salisbury, Chippenham and Bradford on Avon, are considered some of the most beautiful in England, and Castle Combe is arguably the most photographed village in the entire country. Only Swindon, now its own unitary authority, has grown to any great size.

The county has a rich history and, more notably, prehistory. Many of the UK's most important prehistoric monuments are found within Wiltshire. They include Stonehenge, the Avebury stone circle complex and Silbury Hill, the largest prehistoric mound in Europe. A fair number of these monuments are said to be haunted, often by the ancient individuals presumed to be buried there. Wiltshire has a haunted heritage all its own.

This slim volume can only give a hint of the fascinating variety of Wiltshire's ghost-lore. However, within these pages you will encounter ghosts of all types: lords, ladies, humble folk, spectral animals, phantom coaches and even a ghost train.

Many of the county's ghost stories are tied to the English Civil War, with dashing Cavaliers particularly prominent among its apparitions. For some inexplicable reason, there appear to be more ghostly women in the county than there are men. There are also numerous sightings of phantom horses and horsemen and you are just as likely to encounter a ghost on Wiltshire's roads as you are in one of its haunted towns or villages.

After reading this book you may wish to visit the haunted locations for yourself. I would certainly encourage you to do so, for as I have stated above Wiltshire is well blessed with lovely countryside, towns and villages, and they are all worth exploring on their own account. Some of the county's most spectacular sites, including Salisbury Cathedral, Avebury and Longleat, have ghost stories told about them. Wherever you go in Wiltshire, you can be sure that one of the county's many haunted sites will not be far away.

Wiltshire is famous for its ancient monuments and many of them are said to he haunted, including the mysterious mound know as Silbury Hill. iStock

TWO FAMOUS GHOST STORIES

On the very edge of Wiltshire, on the Berkshire border, can be found Littlecote Hall, a handsome Elizabethan manor house now run as a hotel. At one time this was the home of a rotter by the name of William Darrell, known as 'Wild Will'. Wild Will Darrell features in a well-known tale of a horrible murder, some of which, at least, is likely to be true.

According to the legend, a midwife was suddenly summoned in the middle of the night by a masked stranger and taken, blindfolded, to a grand house many miles away. Her blindfold was only removed when she found herself in a luxurious bedchamber in which lay the young woman she had been brought to attend, who was in the last throes of labour. Also in the room was a haughty, imposing man who kept himself aloof from the proceedings.

The midwife helped to deliver a baby boy. Immediately, the man snatched it from her and, to her unspeakable horror, he threw the infant on the fire, raking the coals over it until it was dead. The murderer then left the room, and the midwife did the little she could do to care for and comfort the wretched mother. Too soon she was blindfolded again, led out of the house and taken home. As she was dropped off at her front door, a purse of gold was dropped into her hands as payment for her services and her presumed silence about what she had seen. But she had no intention of letting the murderer get away with his monstrous deed.

While she was being led back out through the mysterious house, the midwife had counted all the steps on the staircase and, more usefully, had cut out a small piece of the bed-curtains in the chamber where the murder had occurred. By estimating the length of time it had taken to transport her there and back, she hoped to be able to narrow down the number of grand houses she could possibly have been taken to. In time the house was identified as Littlecote and suspicion fell upon William Darrell. He was tried at Salisbury for the murder but escaped his sentence by bribing the judge.

However, the legend then states that vengeance came to him from beyond the grave. Shortly after his acquittal, Darrell was thrown from his horse while out hunting and broke his neck. Something had startled his horse, but what? Rumour had it that the phantom of the murdered babe, all wreathed in flames, had suddenly appeared on the path before it. The place where this happened was known for many years as Darrell's Stile and tended to be avoided after dark, for Wild Will himself was still supposed to haunt the spot.

The bedchamber in Littlecote Hall where it was claimed Wild Will Darrell had murdered a child.

In his excellent guide to *The Folklore of Wiltshire*, author Ralph Whitlock states that Wild Will Darrell's ghost would drive up to the door of Littlecote Hall in a spectral carriage whenever an heir to the house was about to die. He continues: 'In about 1861, little Francis Popham, who was six months old, was lying dangerously ill when his nurse heard a coach and horses approaching the house. Thinking that it was the boy's parents, she looked out of the window and saw nothing. That night the child died. His parents did not arrive till the following day.'

A more permanent ghost at Littlecote is that of the tragic mother. As long ago as the 1880s, it was stated that she haunted the bedroom where the murder was committed, 'a woman with dishevelled hair, in white garments, and bearing a babe in her arms'. One source also claims the worthy midwife as a Littlecote ghost. There are many more.

In his book *Haunted Britain*, Antony Hippisley Coxe lists a number of other apparitions seen in and around Littlecote Hall. These include a woman in the garden, another woman in the Chinese room and 'a lady with a rushlight'. He adds: 'Some also believe that a tenant, Gerard Lee Bevin, who rented the place after World War One, and who subsequently served seven years for embezzlement, also haunts the Long Gallery.' To Mr Hippisley Coxe's roster of phantom ladies we can add the one noted by Andrew Green in his *Ghosts of Today*, a figure in an elegant blue gown seen ascending a staircase on the third floor.

In his *Paranormal Wiltshire*, David Scanlan writes that a 'black shrouded figure', perhaps a monk, has also been seen at Littlecote, as well as apparitions that appear to be Roman soldiers. A Roman villa stood very near where the mansion now stands and a section of a beautiful mosaic floor belonging to it can be viewed in the grounds.

A splendidly creepy illustration of Littlecote Hall made in the 19th century.

An extraordinary encounter is recorded by Mr Scanlan as having taken place shortly after Littlecote Hall was bought by entrepreneur Peter de Savary in 1985. According to Mr de Savary, he was in the process of clearing some lumber out of his new property when a woman approached him and called him 'a wicked man'. He asked the woman, whom he had never seen before in his life, what he'd done to deserve such a comment and she told him: 'You have taken my baby's things.'

The stranger then directed him to a small box which contained clothing and other items belonging to her long-deceased children. This he interred in the chapel and the woman was not seen again.

Our second 'most famous' is 'The Demon Drummer of Tedworth', although he – or it – was never seen. Today Tedworth is spelled Tidworth. It is situated on the eastern edge of Salisbury Plain and is a garrison town, as it was in the 1660s, when the 'Drummer' was active.

The story begins with the arrest of a discharged military drummer, one William Drury. Drury was caught with a forged licence granting him permission to play his drum in the street for money. Tidworth was a good place for ex-soldiers on hard times because the town was thronged with military men who might feel some sympathy for him. Unfortunately, Drury made a nuisance of himself, beating his drum all around the town and at all hours of the day and night. When his licence was found to be a fake, he was placed in custody and his drum was confiscated.

Drury was frantic about the removal of his drum but it wasn't returned to him. He was kicked out of Tidworth and the drum found its way to the home of the local magistrate, John Mompesson. If Mompesson had been at home, he would probably have sent it back – it was no good to him, after all – but instead it was dumped in a lumber room. From this point on the series of phenomena which came to be known as the Demon Drummer began to manifest.

For three nights running the house was disturbed by 'a great knocking' on the doors and external walls. It sounded like a gang of thieves had been trying to break in. According to a

An illustration of the Demon Drummer of Tedworth, from the frontispiece of the book which brought the phenomenon to the attention of the public, Saducismus Triumphatus, by Joseph Glanvill. The author experienced the Demon Drummer's activity for himself.

contemporary account (*Saducismus Triumphatus* by Joseph Glanvill): 'After this the noise of thumping and drumming was very frequent. It was on the outside of the house, which is most of it of board. It constantly came as they were going to sleep, whether early or late.'

The sounds were also heard in the room where Drury's drum had been stashed. The disturbances continued for many months and today we would probably label them poltergeist phenomena. In typical poltergeist style, it made the children of the house particular targets. The entity drummed out recognisable rhythms on their bedsteads, but with such violence that everyone expected them to fall apart. Scratching sounds would also be heard. The drumming would pursue children from room to room. The noise was so loud that it could be heard 'three fields away'. Unusually, however loud the noises became, the household dogs were never bothered by them; it was as if they could not even hear them.

After a time, further poltergeist-type behaviour manifested. The Demon Drummer would throw around chairs, shoes 'and every loose thing'. Servants would be dragged out of bed or would feel a great weight on top of them. Mysterious lights were seen about the house. Apparitions also began to be seen. A servant was terrified by a 'great body' looming over his bed, in which were set two 'red and glaring' eyes. Indistinct figures shuffled about the house.

Joseph Glanvill, quoted above, investigated the strange goings-on on behalf of Mr Mompesson. He heard the knocks and scratches for himself and with a friend thoroughly poked about in the various rooms in a vain search for a cause. At one point a disembodied voice spoke to him. He was convinced 'a demon or spirit' was behind the disturbances.

Not everyone shared his opinion, however. For many there was another explanation: that William Drury had cursed the house. One night, a number of men of rank joined the investigations. One of them called out: 'Satan, if the drummer set the work, give three knocks, and no more.' Three distinct knocks were then heard. He then asked, as further confirmation that Drury was behind the disturbances, that they should knock five more times, but then stop for the rest of the night. Five more knocks came and then no more.

A Victorian representation of the Demon Drummer, now reimagined as a ghost wandering Salisbury Plain. iStock

When William Drury was finally tracked down – he was back in gaol but this time in Gloucester on a charge of theft – evidence was presented that he had boasted to a fellow prisoner: 'Do not you hear of the drumming at a gentleman's house at Tedworth? I have plagued him and he shall never be quiet till he hath made me satisfaction for taking away my drum.'

Drury was sentenced to transportation, and the phenomena died down once he was out of the country. So was this a case of a poltergeist infestation, of witchcraft or merely of hysteria? The Demon Drummer remains a fascinating story and one that still asks more questions than it answers.

FOUR HAUNTED HOUSES

Longleat is one of the most magnificent country house estates in England. Situated between Warminster and the border with Somerset, Longleat is a major tourist attraction, not least for its long-established safari park, the first of its kind in Europe. At the heart of the estate is Longleat House, the first stately home in England to open its doors to the public.

Longleat House was built in 1580 and is considered a particularly fine example of Elizabethan architecture. It was built on the site of an Augustinian Priory and replaced an earlier house that had burned down shortly after completion. The new house was designed by its first owner, Sir John Thynne, with input from the top architects of the day. The Thynnes have lived at Longleat ever since the house was built. From the days of Thomas Thynne in the 18th century, the masters of Longleat have held the title of Marquis of Bath, including the current owner, Alexander (who spells his name 'Thynn' after his earliest ancestor, Sir John the Elder, who owned the manor house which burned down).

According to legend, one of this long line of Thynnes returned from the grave and in ghostly form began to visit his widow, to her great distress. The Marquise called in twelve parsons to try to exorcise the troublesome spirit of her late husband. In order to do so, they employed a rather elaborate ritual, as outlined in *The Folklore of the Warminster District* by V.S. Manley:

'A sheepskin was procured, into which the marquise was wrapped, and in a cradle they laid her, and carried her to her room. The twelve parsons sat around a table and waited. At midnight the ghost appeared and stood among them. It begged to be allowed to touch the hem of his wife's garment. They told him this was impossible, because she was wrapped in lamb's wool. Then they walked through the house reciting the Lord's Prayer backwards, which proved effective in ridding the house of the ghost.'

This is a most unusual form of exorcism. Stories of 'ghost-laying' are common throughout the British Isles, but this business of reciting the Lord's Prayer backwards (which sounds somewhat Satanic!) is unique so far as I know, as is the laying of the wife in a cradle. The use of a lamb's skin as a protection against evil is largely confined to Wiltshire, although I have come across one other similar reference in a story from Monmouthshire. The cradle and the lamb skin both appear to be employed as symbols of innocence, the first

Magnificent Longleat House, painted in the 17th century.

of unsullied infancy, the second of the Agnus Dei or Lamb of God. Folklorists Jennifer Westwood and Jacqueline Wilson, in their magnum opus on British traditions, *The Lore of the Land*, wonder whether the Marquise was receiving unwelcome advances (to coin a phrase) from her late husband, a theme which might have been suppressed in later retellings of the story.

Although the defunct Marquis was successfully exorcised, several other ghosts are believed to still haunt Longleat House. The father of the 1st Marquis of Bath was another Thomas Thynne. He held the slightly less grand title of Viscount of Weymouth. He married a woman named Louisa Carteret, but theirs was not a happy union. By all accounts, the Viscount was a cold and forbidding man and Louisa began to look for love elsewhere. She found it with a servant, a footman who had joined the Longleat household on her marriage. Not surprisingly, her husband was furious when he finally got wind of the liaison. The Viscount grabbed the unfortunate footman and, in a towering rage, picked him up and hurled him bodily down the main staircase. He died in the fall, breaking his neck.

It is not the murdered footman, nor his killer, who haunts Longleat, but the sorrowing spirit of Louisa Carteret. Louisa died soon after the death of her lover. Her ghost is described as being either dressed all in grey or in green. She is most often seen wandering forlornly through the passages at the top of the house, where she used to have secret trysts with the footman.

Although he died fifty years before the current house was built, Cardinal Wolsey is also claimed as a ghost for Longleat. Henry VIII's Lord Chancellor before he fell from grace, Wolsey died in exile in 1530. Possibly he visited the Priory which originally stood on the site. The apparition of another senior clergyman, an unidentified bishop, has been seen in the library and the dashing figure of a 17th-century Cavalier has also been spotted from time to time.

A Cavalier is also the ghost of another show home, Lydiard House, near Swindon. Lydiard House was built in the Elizabethan period but was greatly altered in the 18th century to create the stylish Palladian mansion we can enjoy today. The house is hired out as a wedding and conference venue and stands in extensive parkland which is open to the public all year round. No one knows the identity of the Longleat Cavalier, but at Lydiard he is believed to be Sir John, a distinguished member of the St John family, who owned the house for 500 years or so.

Sir John St John was a staunch Royalist during the English Civil War – hence his appearance as a Cavalier, with a showy outfit of highly embroidered clothes, big boots and fancy hat. Of course, the war was won by the opposition, the austere Parliamentarians, and Sir John suffered greatly both before and after the conflict: three of his sons were killed and the Lydiard estate was seized on the orders of Oliver Cromwell. His distinctive ghost has been seen in Lydiard House and patrolling the parkland which was taken from him.

Westwood Manor is a 15th-century house near Bradford on Avon. Although managed by the National Trust, it is only open for a few weeks of the year. Westwood Manor is haunted by that staple of British ghost-lore, a headless ghost. He may represent one of several people who committed suicide in the house shortly after – so it is rumoured – a Gypsy woman placed a curse on it. The woman was the wife of a poacher who was sentenced to be hanged by a magistrate then in residence at Westwood.

Longleat House is haunted by several ghosts and was the scene of a bizarre exorcism. iStock

Near Chippenham can be found Lacock Abbey, a wonderfully antiquated old house whose name gives away its monastic origins. The abbey started life as a nunnery, founded in the 13th century. Like all such institutions, Lacock was closed during Henry VIII's Dissolution of the Monasteries. The abbey was sold to Sir William Sharington, who knocked down the abbey church but converted the main buildings into a private home. His alterations were comparatively minor and the house still demonstrates its medieval monastic origins. It has even retained its original cloisters. However, to an extent this appearance owes something to 18th-century alterations in the Gothic Revival style. The house has been used as a film set for many notable productions, including two of the *Harry Potter* films and the BBC's Tudor drama *Wolf Hall*.

Lacock Abbey is now managed by the National Trust and houses a museum devoted to the house's most famous owner, William Henry Fox Talbot. Fox Talbot was a pioneer in the field of photography. In the 1830s and 1840s he invented methods of photography which directly led to the modern process of capturing an image on negative film. The earliest known negative taken by a camera is a shot of one of the medieval windows in Lacock Abbey. It was taken by Talbot in 1835. In a way, Talbot's photographs can be considered ghosts of the past, capturing forever people and places from long ago.

However, ghosts of the decidedly supernatural sort have also been witnessed at Lacock Abbey, and they are strikingly different in appearance. The first is of a tall, elegant woman with a decidedly aristocratic bearing. Some believe her to be the apparition of the founder of the original nunnery, Lady Ela, the Countess of Salisbury, while others have suggested she may be Lady Sharington, wife of the man who first converted the abbey into a home.

The other ghost encountered at Lacock Abbey couldn't be more different. Two children staying in the house were frightened by 'an ugly little man' who kept appearing in their room. They were allowed to sleep elsewhere and the unwelcome visitor was not seen again. However, when alterations were being carried out some years later, a wall separating the bedroom from the one adjoining was taken down and beneath it was found a skeleton.

The aptly named Kathleen Wiltshire, a keen collector of ghost stories from the county, briefly committed this story to print in her *Ghost Stories of the Wiltshire Countryside*, published in 1973. She does not name the house in Lacock where the incident occurred but later writers have identified it as Lacock Abbey. Kathleen Wiltshire states that all that could be seen of the corpse were two skeletal feet protruding from an older wall,

Lacock Abbey's medieval origins are immediately apparent.
The origins of its two very different ghosts are more obscure. iStock

adding: 'The owners of the house were away and the builders simply rebuilt the wall without finding out what exactly was hidden.' However, in more recently published books we learn of a 'dwarfish skeleton' or one of a 'deformed man', linking the remains more firmly with the apparition.

TWO CREEPY CASTLES

Wardour Castle (also known as Old Wardour Castle), near Tisbury, has a chequered history and now only the shell of it remains. The castle was built in the 15th century in a unique six-sided design. Originally owned by the Lovell family, it was confiscated by Henry Tudor because of their loyalty to Richard III, and after a time passed into the hands of Sir Thomas Arundell. It was confiscated again when Sir Thomas was beheaded for allegedly fomenting a plot to overthrow the government of King Henry VIII.

Sir Thomas's son was allowed to buy back the castle, however, and the Arundells remained in possession until the English Civil War. A staunchly Catholic family, they took the side of King Charles against the Parliamentarians. The most exciting moment in its history took place when the 61-year-old Lady Blanche Arundell found herself besieged by Cromwell's forces in 1643. Her husband was away from home on business for the king when a 1,300-strong army of Roundheads arrived at her gates. With only 25 soldiers at her command, the plucky lady refused to allow them entrance and they immediately laid siege to the castle. Lady Arundell held out for five days, but by this time the Roundheads had armed themselves with explosives and were preparing to undermine the walls, so she capitulated.

A view from Wardour Castle down to the lake, where the ghost of Lady Arundell has been seen. iStock

In the meantime, Lord Arundell had been killed fighting for the king. But his son Henry then besieged his own castle and successfully ousted the Parliamentarians who had taken possession of it. After he started blowing up sections of his home with gunpowder, the garrison gave up and Wardour Castle was returned to him, albeit in rather poor shape. It never really recovered its former glory. In the 18th century a new house in the Palladian style was built nearby – New Wardour Castle. The old castle was kept on as an ornamental feature in the surrounding park and is today in the care of English Heritage.

Old Wardour Castle is haunted by a female apparition, assumed to be the dauntless Lady Arundell. She has most often been observed at twilight, walking from the castle ruins down the hill to the lake in the grounds, but she is also known to haunt the ruins themselves.

Another creepy story is associated with the Arundells of Wardour Castle. Family legend had it that the appearance of white owls would presage the death of an Arundell, and this was apparently the case just before the death of the last of the line in 1944.

Like Wardour Castle, the fortress at Devizes also suffered in the Civil War, but rather more so. Devizes Castle was a Royalist stronghold, holding out against one siege by Parliamentarians but finally falling in 1645 when Oliver Cromwell himself invaded the town and brought with him heavy artillery to smash the castle walls. Three years later the castle was 'slighted', in other words dismantled, to ensure it could never again be used by the Royalists. Now nothing remains of the medieval castle other than the motte and bailey mound raised by the Normans in the 11th century. Taking its place, however, is a vast Victorian house designed to look like a medieval castle. The house, which is private property, is certainly an excellent facsimile, with its massive walls and castellated towers.

This Devizes Castle has now been converted into flats, and a number of its residents have reported spooky experiences over the years. Once again, a Cavalier is numbered among the ghosts. He has been encountered on a staircase, striking a pose in his uniform, a feather sticking out of his broad-brimmed hat. Presumably the stair he stands on corresponds with a stair or floor level in the original castle. Dating from a more modern age is the apparition of a little old lady who has been seen pottering round the entrance hall, leaning on a stick.

Another female phantom, a beautiful young girl, also haunts Devizes Castle. Local legend insists she is Isabella of Valois, the wife of King Richard II, who spent some time in the medieval fortress in the 14th century. According to the story, the King discovered that Isabella had been unfaithful to him and in revenge had her walled up in the castle, so that she suffered a slow and agonising death from hunger or starvation. The tale is utter nonsense, however. Isabella was married at the age of six and became a widow at the age of nine when Richard was murdered on the orders of Henry Bolingbroke (who then crowned himself Henry IV). Isabella was the daughter of the King and Queen of France and the marriage was a purely political alliance. It is known that she returned to France after Richard's downfall and several years later married again. Sadly, she died in childbirth at the still tender age of nineteen.

The identity of this ghost of Devizes Castle is therefore still in doubt. Perhaps some other unfortunate suffered the horrible fate attributed to Isabella and that is her reason for haunting the site.

Haunted Devizes Castle is a grand Victorian house in the medieval style which replaced a castle torn down during the Civil War.

GHOSTS AROUND TOWN

Swindon has long been the largest town in Wiltshire and has grown so much that it has been given its own unitary authority status. Swindon was a modest market town until the 1840s, after which it began to undergo considerable expansion due at first to the construction of two canals and then the Great Western Railway. The Industrial Revolution had fuelled the need for convenient transportation routes and Swindon's success was assured when Isambard Kingdom Brunel chose the town for the location of a GWR locomotive repair works. A 'Railway Village' was rapidly developed to house workers, and this remains a key area of Swindon today. The picturesque heart of the original market town is now known as Old Town.

Swindon has a number of interesting haunted locations. The Wyvern Theatre, for example, is said to have a haunted lift, which has the unnerving habit of zooming up and down of its own accord. Staff have reported feeling an eerie presence around the stage and of seeing 'black figures' here and in the auditorium. The sound of someone running down a corridor in the administration area has also proved a puzzle.

Running footsteps are also a feature of the odd goings-on reported from another modern building, Swindon's Central Fire Station. Whoever is causing them has proved equally elusive. Several apparitions have been sighted over the years, including one described as 'an old lock-keeper' and another resembling a drowned woman.

The Health Hydro, a spa and swimming pool complex housed within a grand Victorian building, is another unusual haunted location. A ghost affectionately known as 'Arthur' patrols the Hydro and on one occasion a member of staff heard a disembodied female voice politely ask him out of empty air: 'What are you doing here?' The South West Paranormal Group witnessed a number of inexplicable goings-on during a vigil here, including a light turning itself off or on according to the wishes of the investigators.

The Clifton public house in Old Town is supposedly built on the site of a priory or convent, explaining its haunting by a spectral nun. Poltergeist activity has also been known to break out in the pub from time to time. A number of apparitions have been reported from The Jolly Tar, a former farmhouse in the suburb of Hannington. They include a woman seen sitting in a chair in the bar and a man 'in old-fashioned clothes' standing by a fireplace. It is either this ghost or 'an old lady' which is seen walking out of the fireplace, depending on which source you read. When The Jolly Tar was investigated by Swindon's own respected ghost researchers, the Paranormal Site Investigators (PSI), they heard bangs emanating from a storeroom which was found to be empty, and members also glimpsed possible apparitions, one of a figure 'dipping down' into this storeroom, and others of people apparently peering into the bar but who were unable to be found when followed.

Swindon, the most populated place in Wiltshire, boasts several unusual haunted locations. iStock

Haunted Swindon, by **PSI** members Dave Wood and Nicky Sewell, provides an excellent overview of the town's hauntings as well as details of the team's many careful investigations over the years, and is highly recommended.

After Swindon, Chippenham is the second largest settlement in Wiltshire. A phantom horseman is said to haunt the grounds of St Margaret's Convent near Chippenham Community Hospital. The handsome Bear Hotel in the town's marketplace is believed to stand on the site of a medieval convent, and a bricked-up archway in the cellar is rumoured to have behind it a tunnel leading to Lacock Abbey. A chambermaid walking to work in the Bear distinctly saw a woman in grey open a window above her and then lean out of it. Curious, she hurried up to the room but found it empty, and the window still fastened. She learned that the room had not been occupied that day or the night before. It is possible she had seen a ghost of a nun. On another occasion a former landlord heard raised voices coming from a bedroom, but when he entered it, he found it unoccupied.

Spooky goings-on were recently reported as manifesting in an ordinary terrace house in Chippenham. The owner told the BBC: 'We get various things happening, like lights going on and off and people running up and down stairs. We also hear voices and my son wakes up in the night saying there's someone sitting on the end of his bed.'

The family blamed the phenomena on the spirit of a man they named 'Kristoff', whose appearance, they believed, could be seen mysteriously reproduced on a bedroom wall. They described the marks as representing 'quite a dirty face, a sort of bearded face, long finger-nails, dirty hands ... a heavy coat, quite a mature man'. Despite his rather unsavoury appearance, they were convinced 'Kristoff' was a benign presence, but they called in a medium to help him move on, and the strange phenomena quietened down soon afterwards.

Kathleen Wiltshire refers to a strange superstition about the town in her book *Ghosts and Legends of the Wiltshire Countryside*. She writes: 'A house in Chippenham has the unlucky reputation that should any young woman who is pregnant look out into the street from a certain window, she will have an unaccountable urge to throw herself down into the street below. It is said these rooms were once occupied by a lady of easy virtue who was said to have many "friends" – chiefly farmers – who visited her on market days. She eventually found herself "in a certain condition" and threw herself to her death from the window of her room. Her uneasy spirit is said

A view of the Market Place in Chippenham, as it appeared in 1820.
The haunted Bear Hotel is on the right.

to enter any woman in that condition and urge her to do the same.'

The city of Salisbury is world famous for its majestic cathedral. Salisbury Cathedral was built in the 13th century and is a splendid example of the Early English Gothic style of architecture. It has the tallest spire of any church in Britain. It also has the largest cloisters and the largest close of any English cathedral. In addition, it contains the world's oldest working clock and the best preserved copy of the *Magna Carta*.

A spooky legend is attached to Salisbury Cathedral. It starts with a bishop who died abroad in the year 1414. A great flock of unknown white birds flew out of the sky and settled on the roof of the building in which his body was lying in state. They made quite a clamour all night and no one recalled ever having seen or heard anything quite like them before. From then on, according to the legend, mysterious white birds will be seen in the vicinity of the cathedral whenever its incumbent bishop is about to die.

The 'tradition' may have started as recently as 1885, however, for it was then that Annie Moberley, daughter of the bishop at the time, saw two white birds flap out of the palace gardens while her father lay dying. The author Edith Oliver, herself a keen collector of Wiltshire folklore, claimed to have had a similar experience in 1911. She saw two 'very large white birds' soaring across a neighbouring meadow on the day the bishop died. Stranger still, the birds were flying without moving their wings.

Within Salisbury Cathedral, a weird apparition has been reported above the tomb of Charles, 8th Baron Stourton. This 16th-century aristocrat was convicted of the murder of two

Salisbury Cathedral rises majestically above the city. Several strange traditions belong to the cathedral. iStock

men and was hanged in 1557. For many years a noose was suspended above the tomb as a grim reminder to visitors of the Baron's crime. My guess is that this was a concession to allow his body to be interred within the cathedral, for murderers were usually denied burial in consecrated ground. The Baron's noble status may have encouraged this compromise. The shadowy form of a noose is said to still be glimpsed from time to time, dangling above the tomb as it did centuries ago.

Before the building of the 13th-century edifice, an earlier cathedral stood just outside modern Salisbury on top of a hill called Old Sarum. Old Sarum was a thriving community for hundreds of years, occupying a site inhabited since at least the Iron Age. However, it became too cramped and it was decided to move the cathedral, and ultimately the entire settlement, to the plain below. Little remains on Old Sarum now other than a series of circular ramparts and a few stones from the original cathedral. The site is in the care of English Heritage and open to the public.

'Time slips' – not just ghosts but visions of an earlier age – have been reported from Old Sarum. One woman who visited the site in the 1960s claimed: 'Once I and others saw a sort of village street, all sunshine, trees and old tiled roofs. It was perfectly clear and natural-looking but it was not there.' The witness added that on another occasion she saw what appeared to be the apparition of a boy of the Saxon period on Old Sarum. He was swinging from the branch of a yew tree growing on the outer ramparts. She described the child as being dressed in 'a rough tunic, and short cloak, both brown, and lighter-coloured leggings or hose, criss-crossed with thongs to the knee.'

Returning to Salisbury, the city's elegant Guildhall has two ghosts. One is of an unidentified man who paces the corridors, especially the area near the old cells. It is possible he was a prisoner here at one time. The other is a woman in a white gown. Her presence is even more puzzling. Was she the bride of some young man imprisoned or sentenced to death here many years ago?

The Haunch of Venison bar and restaurant in Minster Street is Salisbury's oldest inn. It is constructed of wattle and daub and is known to have accommodated men working on the building of the cathedral spire in 1320. At one time, according to the restaurant's website, the building was used as a brothel and a tunnel was made so that clergymen from nearby St Thomas's Church could visit it without embarrassment! There is also a tradition that Churchill and Eisenhower used a discreet bar – originally set aside for women – in the upper storey of the building to plan the D-Day landings.

The traditional ghost of the Haunch of Venison is a woman in a white or grey gown who has been seen to stare out of the windows overlooking St Thomas's churchyard. One source suggests she is a grieving mother looking for a lost child. Unexplained footsteps have also been detected pacing the top floor between 11.30pm and midnight. In the so-called 'House of Lords' upstairs bar (reserved for the Higher Clergy once upon a time) there can be found a grisly relic. On display in an antiquated oven is what appears to be a mummified hand. The tale told about it is that it belonged to a man who was caught cheating at cards, and was hacked off in a drastic act of retribution. It was supposedly discovered in the 19th century but may well be a modern prop. Either way, the restless spirit

Earthworks and low walls are all that remain of the once thriving community of Old Sarum but there are claims that some people have been afforded glimpses of its Saxon past. iStock

of the card cheat is also said to haunt the Haunch of Venison and is blamed for any odd events, such as glasses moving or falling and beer taps turning themselves off and on.

Malmesbury is a historic market town which can also boast the distinction of being England's oldest borough, created in 880 by Alfred the Great. The jewel in its crown is Malmesbury Abbey, founded in the 7th century and considered one of the great centres of learning in the Middle Ages. At one time it housed the second biggest library in Europe. William of Malmesbury, one of medieval England's most important scholars, was resident here in the 12th century and he tells a remarkable tale of a monk who made an early attempt at manned flight by jumping off one of the abbey's towers with wings attached to his arms. He survived the fall but broke both his legs in the attempt. The abbey was also notable for possessing the first ever church organ in England, installed in the early 700s.

Malmesbury Abbey was a much grander building than is visible today and at one time possessed a spire even taller than Salisbury Cathedral's. Nevertheless, it has fared better than most monastic houses during the Dissolution of the Monasteries under Henry VIII. It was closed down but escaped being flattened to make way for agriculture or converted into a private home, as was usually the case. Instead, its central core was retained for worship and was made the parish church. This gives the abbey a slightly lopsided appearance, with ruinous arches and incomplete walls stretching out from the surviving Norman nave.

The ghost of a black-habited Benedictine monk has been glimpsed from time to time in the abbey's cemetery. The

Echoes of monkish days can be both seen and heard at Malmesbury Abbey.
iStock

sounds of chanting and singing have also been heard emanating from the abbey after dark.

Opposite Malmesbury Abbey is the Old Bell Hotel, which was built in 1220 to accommodate scholars who had come to peruse the books and manuscripts in the Abbey's famous library. As such, the Old Bell is considered the oldest purpose-built hotel in the UK. It is haunted by a Grey Lady, who is believed to be the very same woman who is portrayed in a painting in the restaurant. Dating from the early 1900s, the painting shows its subject wearing a grey gown. Staff will tell you that the lady was jilted on her wedding day and has haunted the hotel ever since. She waited in vain at the abbey for her beloved to arrive and was then coaxed away to the Old Bell, where she continued to wait for the errant groom to turn up, pacing the corridors in growing despair. Her spirit is now supposed to continue wandering miserably through the hotel as she did on that unhappy day.

A director of the hotel informed author of *Paranormal Wiltshire*, David Scanlan, of a recent sighting. He told him: 'A guest from the United States of America … got up in the middle of the night to go to the toilet and started to have a conversation with what he thought was his wife. When he returned to the bed he noticed his wife was still asleep. I remember the man came running downstairs in a bit of a scared state. He checked out the following morning.'

Kathleen Wiltshire has an alternative explanation for the Grey Lady, however. She states that when alterations were being carried out at the Old Bell in 1889, an underground passage, apparently constructed in Norman times, was discovered and in them was a quantity of human bones, including the skeleton

The Old Bell at Malmesbury, seen from the Abbey churchyard. Is the mysterio Grey Lady of the Old Bell now buried in the churchyard? iStock

of a woman, standing upright. The tradition of walled-up nuns sprang to mind as a possible explanation for the Grey Lady. The skeleton was interred in the Abbey churchyard, but this clearly did not prevent her ghost from walking, if indeed the bones did belong to her. Mrs Wiltshire adds that the Grey Lady has been seen outside the hotel. The apparition was always seen walking in the same direction, passing through a hedge as it did so. That patch of the hedge always died, no matter how often it was replanted.

The King's Arms Hotel in the High Street isn't quite as old as the Old Bell – it merely dates back to the reign of Good Queen Bess! This venerable coaching inn is said to be haunted by Harry Jones, who was its landlord for forty years, from 1880 to 1920. In the bedroom where he died the eerie sound of heavy breathing has been heard by a number of witnesses.

Another defunct landlord is believed to haunt a pub in one of Wiltshire's prettiest towns. Bradford on Avon is an attractive jumble of buildings constructed of mellow Cotswold stone. In addition to the River Avon, the town is watered by the Kennet and Avon Canal, beside which stands the Canal Tavern. The apparition of an elderly fellow puffing on an old clay pipe has sometimes been seen in a room which at one time served as the pub's kitchen. He looks so much at home that it is thought he is the shade of a past publican.

Bradford on Avon's oldest building is St Laurence's Church, a tiny place of worship dating back to the Saxon period. A congregation of men and women in medieval dress have been seen entering St Laurence's. A clergyman once saw a vision of what he described as 'a phantom leper colony' at the church.

St Laurence's stands in the shadow of the town's parish church, Holy Trinity. In a cottage overlooked by Holy Trinity Church an unusual haunting once took place. A young woman heard on several successive nights a sound like coins being jingled together, followed by the appearance of the shadowy figure of a man. The apparition would stand in her bedroom for a few moments before melting away. Sometime later the cottage was taken by another family. The tenant sleeping in this same room also saw the ghost and was so frightened that he took his bed downstairs, refusing to sleep there again.

When the house was subsequently undergoing a scheme of modernisation, a skeleton was found buried in a shallow grave under a flagstone. This hasty burial suggested a victim of murder and therefore an explanation for the haunting. Hopes that the sound of jingling coins might point to treasure also being hidden about the premises were not realised, however.

The ancient town of Wilcot – many centuries ago Wiltshire's county town – is haunted by the unfortunate 'Dame Anne', the young wife of a former squire of Stowell Park. Her husband wrongly accused Anne of infidelity and kicked her out of the house on Christmas Eve during a snowstorm. The poor woman struggled through the snow down a lane now called Nanny's Lane and tried to make her way to the neighbouring village of Cocklebury for shelter. But she died of exposure before she could reach safety and her frozen body was found on Christmas Day. Her apparition is seen in Nanny's Lane wearing a long, white gown.

A horrible apparition has been encountered on a footpath on the outskirts of Melksham. It appears innocuous enough at first, simply a man carrying an umbrella. However, it then blocks the path, ignoring requests for it to stand aside. Finally,

Several unusual hauntings have been reported from the picturesque town of Bradford on Avon. iStock

when the frustrated pedestrian is forced to try and push past, the figure reacts. It raises its umbrella threateningly and only then does the shocked witness realise that it has no head, just a stump of a neck. There is no story to account for this gruesome spectre, but it may be significant that it appears at a place where a stile, known as the Devil's Stile, formerly stood. Stiles were traditionally considered to be places visited by ghosts.

A much more benign apparition has been seen in the King's Arms in Melksham: that of a little girl. She appeared in a bedroom, dripping wet, or so it seemed. According to the witness, the apparition 'looked like a black and white photo'. Her identity is unknown but the wet-through state of the child suggests she may have drowned or died after catching a chill during a downpour.

Another haunted pub can be found in Warminster. Many years ago a landlady at the Masons Arms shot herself for reasons unknown and it is thought to be this unhappy soul who now haunts the pub. Nicknamed Mary, she has the annoying habit of pushing glasses off the shelves in the bar so that they smash. Her apparition has recently been seen descending a spiral staircase. The phantom of a man has also been glimpsed on the pub's upper storey.

By an odd coincidence, another Wiltshire pub has a spiral staircase haunted by a phantom female. This elegantly dressed ghost is seen ascending the spiral staircase in the Royal Oak, Corsham, flicking her long dress coquettishly as she does so.

In his book *The Folklore of Wiltshire*, Ralph Whitlock states that in the 1940s two children were left in the care of a housekeeper at Corsham Priory, in Priory Street, while their parents were out of the country. When the parents returned they found that one of the children had learned the Ave Maria, not from the Protestant housekeeper, but from 'a man in white' who used to appear to the boy. Two hundred years before, the Priory had been occupied by a religious order who dressed in white.

Corsham's fine medieval church, St Bartholomew's is said to be haunted by a weird entity, a tiny and malevolent man just a couple of feet tall. It's possible he started off in the local folklore as some sort of goblin but increasingly became considered to be a ghost over the centuries as the belief in fairies faded.

A phantom bell-ringer is the ghost of St Mary's Church, Calne. The church has eight bells. On a few occasions when only seven ringers have turned up, the campanologists have heard footsteps mounting the stone steps up to the tower. They've assumed it's the missing ringer arriving at last but no one is to be seen. A bend in a lane at Calne is named Scots Corner after a Scotsman who was murdered here. His ghost, distinctively wearing a kilt, has been seen in the lane.

We have already visited Devizes Castle. In the town's Market Place is another historic building, the elegant 18th-century Black Swan Hotel. The hotel has long had a reputation for ghostly goings-on. The apparition of a young woman in a long, flowing dress has been spotted in a number of places throughout the hotel. She has a gauzy, transparent appearance and has been known to walk through walls. Something described as a 'shadowy figure', apparently not the same ghost, has been glimpsed gliding through the reception area and then down the steps leading to the cellar. Heavy doors leading into the function room have the habit of opening and closing by themselves and mysterious footsteps have also been heard in the hotel.

The Wiltshire Museum is based in Devizes. Among its many artefacts exploring the long history – and indeed prehistory – of the county is a desk which belonged to Maud Cunnington, a prominent archaeologist who helped to excavate West Kennet Long Barrow (see 'Avebury and Beyond'). Although the museum officers doubt the story, there is a persistent rumour that the shade of Maud Cunnington has been seen sitting at her old desk, as if still engaged in her important work.

Finally, we come to Marlborough, which is said to be haunted by the ghost of a highwayman, possibly the notorious William

An old print of Devizes Market Place, home of the haunted Black Swan Hotel

Boulter, who was born in Poulshot in 1748 and hanged at the age of 30 after a busy life of banditry. His ghost gallops

through the town and then through the grounds of Marlborough College. Sometimes only the thunder of his horse's hooves are heard. The phantom appears to be following the route of an old road, now overgrown. Whether the highwayman is racing to meet a coach in time to hold it up or is fleeing the scene of a crime is open to conjecture.

An extraordinary encounter with a departed spirit allegedly took place in Marlborough in 1674. A weaver named Thomas Goddard gave a statement under oath to the Mayor, the Town Clerk and the Rector of St Peter's Church that he had been accosted by the spirit of his dead father-in-law, Edward Avon, while he was walking to work one morning. Avon's ghost told

Goddard that he wanted to present his daughter, Goddard's wife, with some money because he had been so tight-fisted in life (or to put it in his own words, that he had 'shut his bowels of compassion toward her'). He had twenty or thirty silver shillings in his hand but the weaver was too scared to accept the money. Recognising that Goddard was afraid, Avon's spirit agreed to appear on another occasion.

So followed a series of visits from the defunct Avon to his son-in-law, who did everything he could to avoid trafficking with the spirit, the lure of a cash reward notwithstanding. The ghost persecuted poor Goddard with all sorts of instructions, to return this and that and to make gifts of money to this person or the other. One of the most important commissions was to take a sword belonging to Avon into a wood, and to carry out the task Goddard took with him his brother-in-law

In the 17th century Marlborough was the scene of a remarkable statement to the authorities regarding the repeated appearances of a ghost. iStock

William Avon for support. On this occasion Edward Avon's spirit was accompanied by a huge, spectral dog. The ghost indicated a spot on the forest floor in which to thrust the sword. Having done so, the two men were told that this marked the place where Avon had murdered a man from whom he had taken money (presumably unlawfully).

'What would you have me do in this thing?' asked Goddard. The ghost replied: 'This is that the world may know that I murdered a man and buried him in this place in the year 1635.' That was the last Thomas Goddard, or anyone else, saw of the ghost of Edward Avon.

HAUNTED VILLAGES

Although the towns may have the lion's share of the ghost stories from Wiltshire, thanks to their larger populations, many of its villages are no less haunted. Castle Combe is one of Wiltshire's prettiest and most photographed villages. It is the archetypal Cotswolds village, a collection of picturesque stone cottages built of mellow golden stone. The ancient bridge over the River Bybrook, the jumble of houses and the charming little church beyond create a scene that has graced numerous jigsaws and chocolate boxes over the years.

On the edge of the village can be found the medieval Castle Combe Manor House, now a hotel. This handsome building is haunted by a Grey Lady who may date from the time of the Norman castle – after which the village is named – that originally stood on the site. Hers is a quiet haunting, drifting peacefully through the hotel, intent on her own paranormal business.

Castle Combe resides in the bottom of a steep, wooded valley. Overlooking the village are the Parsonage Woods where the sounds of a ghostly battle are to be heard; the clashing of swords and the savage cries of fighting men. Author Rupert Matthews believes these may be the echo of a scrap between Viking invaders and a hastily assembled band of Saxon defenders in the 9th century. No less a personage than Alfred Great led the Saxon force, but they were greatly outnumbered and, after a valiant effort, had to withdraw to fight another day. Eventually, Alfred met the Danish commander, Guthrum, again and this time was victorious, forcing him to convert to Christianity before sending him packing.

In common with Castle Combe, the castle which gave its name to the village of Castle Eaton, near Swindon, is long since gone but it does have a Grade I-listed Norman church with an important medieval preaching cross in its graveyard. The venerable Red Lion Inn is the haunted building here. Its ghost is unlikely ever to be identified, for it has no face. The 'Faceless Man', as he has understandably become known, is dressed in dark clothing with silver buckles on his shoes. In the past the ghost has made its presence known by thumping up and down a flight of stairs, causing sudden drops in temperature and throwing objects about, including a clock, which launched itself from a wall in front of several witnesses. On one occasion the landlady was woken up by the Faceless Man shaking her by the shoulder. He loomed over her bed but did not speak – how could he without a mouth? – and then vanished.

We have already visited a number of haunted pubs in Wiltshire, and there are others. On the western limits of the county is the picturesque village of Monkton Farleigh. Who would have thought that such a perfect picture of tranquillity would have had hidden below it a huge storehouse full of bombs and guns? This occurred during World War II, when mines beneath the village were used as secret armaments depot.

Like the rest of Monkton Farleigh, its inn, formerly the King's Arms but now renamed the Muddy Duck, is built out of Bath Stone. One of its ghosts is one of the miners who slaved underground to free this valuable material from the earth. The inn was built as a private home, replacing a Cluniac Priory which was shut down during the reign of Henry VIII. Its

The 14th-century Castle Combe Manor House Hotel is haunted by a Grey Lady.
iStock

second ghost is the shade of one of the monks who worshipped here centuries ago. Also reported from the pub is the sorrowful weeping of a woman who lost her life when the coach she was travelling in crashed outside.

Nearer Bradford on Avon, at Avoncliff, is the Cross Guns, said to be haunted by both a Grey Lady and a Blue Lady, but one may be the indistinct appearance of the other. At Wanborough, at the foot of the Marlborough Downs, the delightfully old-world Harrow Inn is still visited by a regular customer from a past age, a coachman by the name of Old Marlow.

The White Horse Inn, in Downton, south of Salisbury, has roots dating back to the Middle Ages and used to face a gallows where local criminals were hanged. According to village tradition, many of those about to be executed were allowed one last drop at the White Horse before they suffered the fatal drop on the scaffold.

A range of inexplicable phenomena has been reported from here, including the smashing of glasses by an unseen hand also reported from the Masons Arms in Warminster (see previous chapter). Mysterious faces have been observed peering out of windows and a phantom woman at one time haunted one of the bedrooms. Landlord Paul Whitburn told ghost researcher David Scanlan of a strange sighting he had to the rear of the inn, facing an old stable block converted for use as a function room.

He explained: 'It was about 4.30am and I was in the beer garden when I saw this strange little orange ball come out of the stable block, bounce four times along the ground and then zip straight back into the stables. I remember it glowed but it didn't emit any ambient light of its own.'

A rather unlikely tale is also told of this stable block. A dairy maid was allegedly drowned in a vat of milk by a man with whom she had had a violent disagreement.

In Wiltshire ghosts of women appear to be more common than those of men. The apparition of an unknown woman has been seen coming through the gates of a big house in Bulford and then crossing the road which runs through the village. Once on the other side of the road, she walks straight through a fence and disappears from view. Another ghostly woman is seen on the road just outside Potterne. She is dressed in green with a dark collar on her jacket. This ghost has even been known to accept lifts from passing motorists, but vanishes once inside the car.

St Mary's Church, Rodbourne Cheney, is haunted by a woman said to have been hanged for murdering her baby. Her melancholy figure wanders the graveyard in search of the child. Another female figure has been seen in St Mary's Church, Purton. In 1872 a woman's skeleton, thought to be that of a nun, was discovered during alteration work in the church and the ghost was naturally linked to it.

Finally, there is a particularly well-attested haunting from Highworth, north of Swindon. This account of a particularly creepy apparition in St Michael's Church is to be found in a classic work on the supernatural, *Apparitions and Haunted Houses*, by Sir Ernest Bennett, published in 1939. Listed as 'Case 59', the author quotes a letter from a young man named J. Graham Arkell:

'I was in the church with my brother (fifteen) and sister (eighteen) and a friend (eighteen). We were at the organ when Miss Ludlow (the friend aforesaid) suddenly said, "Oh look! Whatever is that?" We all turned and saw down by the church door (south) the figure of a man, leaning forward, apparently interested in what we were singing. What struck us all simultaneously was that instead of having an ordinary face, the figure had a featureless grey blank, though where the eyes should have been there were sunken dark shadows. The others were rather horrified and turned away, but I still looked on until it disappeared behind a pillar with a jerky movement of the arms.

'A lady who was decorating the font down by the same door at the same time saw nothing and said no one had been into the church. The sun was shining at the time (11.30am) so that we could not have mistaken it for any ordinary person, as it was by the open door where the light was very bright. This is the barest statement and gives no idea of the horrible impression made upon the persons.'

The letter was dated a few days after the sighting. Sir Ernest Bennett received a tip-off that the ghost had also been seen by the verger of St Michael's Church, who wrote back in response to his inquiry of what he had seen one evening in November 1936, at about 7.45 pm. 'I had just unlocked the church to light up for choir practice and as I turned round from closing the door, the figure came up the centre aisle and went through some curtains near the west end door; it did not appear to part them, but went straight through them. The only

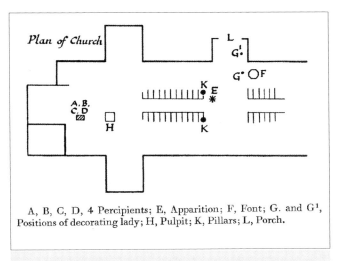

An illustration from Sir Ernest Bennett's Apparitions and Haunted Houses of the interior plan of Highworth Church and the people present when they saw a ghost (see the key – 'E' is the ghost).

light was from the lamps out in town, so it was rather dark, so I could not discern any features; it was medium height and dressed in a long white robe, it made no noise as it glided along.'

The apparition has also been seen entering the church from Sheep Street. It glides past the Church House, through the churchyard gate and then vanishes through the vestry door. No explanation has come forward as to the identity of the ghost.

AVEBURY AND BEYOND

Avebury is certainly one of Wiltshire's most fascinating villages. At its centre, adjacent to the church, is its Elizabethan manor house, barely altered since the 16th century and now managed by the National Trust. There are a number of spooky stories about Avebury Manor. On one occasion an au pair saw a monk in a black habit sitting in the library. She assumed he was a guest and asked another servant if she should lay a place for him at lunch. She was told there was no such guest in the house and when they looked back into the library the monk had vanished. Avebury Manor is built on the site of a 12th-century Benedictine monastery. The Benedictine Order wore black habits.

A Cavalier – that most ubiquitous of Wiltshire ghosts – has been seen wandering round the house and garden. A young woman staying in the house saw him from her bedroom window and was startled by his extraordinary outfit. She rushed down to the garden but he was nowhere to be seen. The Cavalier is thought to be the ghost of a former owner of Avebury Manor, the Royalist Sir John Stawell, who was ruined after the Parliamentarians won the Civil War. An odd phenomenon, possibly connected to this ghost, has been reported from the so-called Crimson Room in the Manor House. On certain mornings all the windows in the room have been found to be open and rose petals are scattered all over the floor. Kathleen Wiltshire thinks the Crimson Room may well have been the one from which the Cavalier was seen.

In addition, a spectral coach-and-four has been seen passing the manor house's gates. This may be the same phantom which is said to haunt the Red Lion Inn in the village. It is never seen at the inn, however, but merely heard rattling up outside. The pub also lays claim to another ghost, known as 'Florrie'. A tale is told to explain this presence. Florrie is said to have lived at the Red Lion during the English Civil War. When her husband left her to take part in the fighting, flirty Florrie lost no time in finding a lover. Unfortunately, the couple were caught out when the absent husband returned unexpectedly. The enraged soldier drew his sword and stabbed his rival to death without a word. Then he turned his fury on his faithless wife, choking the life out of her with his bare hands.

Florrie is now the most persistent ghost at the Red Lion. She is blamed for any odd happenings, such as objects moving or going missing and beer taps inexplicably switching themselves off and on. The pub has become popular with paranormal investigation groups. Their visits have added a growing roster of ghosts to keep Florrie company. David Scanlan lists them in his *Paranormal Wiltshire*. They include: 'The phantom of an old lady, the spirits of children playing on a landing, a man wearing a hat sitting in the bar [and] a lady sitting in one of the rooms apparently writing a letter.'

Elsewhere in Avebury, a ghostly woman has been seen standing by a gate on the footpath leading to the neighbouring village of Avebury Trusloe. She has been described as 'looking like a nun', in a white hood. Her gown is finely decorated with lace, however, which sounds too fancy for a nun. An official with the old Ministry of Works had a close encounter with this ghost one morning. She stepped into his path, took him by the shoulders and gently turned him to walk in the opposite direction. Disembodied footsteps, apparently belonging to somebody male, have been heard tramping up the minor road through Avebury Trusloe

Avebury Manor is haunted by a monk, a Cavalier and a spectral coach
iStock

The world-famous stone circle complex at Avebury is an extraordinary structure: three rings of monoliths behind a massive ditch with 'avenues' of stones leading into and out of them, originally for miles. The stones were set up in the Neolithic period, at about the same time as the pyramids were built in Egypt. One can only guess at the elaborate rituals that would once have taken place here.

Only a small proportion of the monoliths erected by Stone Age man remain in place, but even this is remarkable considering their great antiquity. For centuries they were probably regarded with superstitious dread, and this may have helped preserve them. When the village of Avebury grew up in the Middle Ages, some of the monoliths were dragged away for use as building stone, while others were buried *in situ*, perhaps to remove any devilish power they were thought to possess. When these stones were being returned to their upright positions by archaeologists in the 1930s, the crushed body of a man was found lying beneath one of them. He had lain there since the 14th century. This tragedy may have helped prevent further destruction of the stone circle.

Over the years a number of strange apparitions have been reported from the Avebury monuments. One bright, moonlit night in the 1960s, a Miss Dunn was driving along the road which cuts through the stone circle when she noticed small figures moving among the stones. She immediately felt there was something uncanny about them. Almost as soon as she began to observe them, however, they vanished. Miss Dunn wondered whether she had been granted a brief glimpse of an earlier time, when the stones were still being used for prehistoric rituals. The people of ancient Britain were much smaller in size than we are today.

Decades earlier the Wiltshire author Edith Olivier also experienced a surprising vision among the Avebury stones. She was approaching the village early one evening, thinking she might stretch her legs for a while, when she saw a cavalcade of lights within the circle. The sounds of music and the mingled voices of a crowd reached her. Thinking that a fair must be going on in the village, Mrs Olivier decided to continue on her drive to Marlborough, her hopes of a quiet stroll frustrated. Back home she mentioned that a fair was taking place at Avebury but was told that this was impossible: no such event had been held in the village for decades. She concluded that what she had seen and heard must have been a ghost, some sort of echo from the past.

On the edge of the village of Avebury is the remarkable structure known as Silbury Hill. Standing 130 feet (40 metres) in height, Silbury Hill is the largest man-made mound in Europe and overlooks the stone circle. It is considered to be part of the same Stone Age 'ritual landscape' but its purpose remains a mystery. It was presumed to be a gigantic burial mound, raised above some powerful king or priest of ancient times, but repeated investigations both unauthorized and professional have failed to find anything within it besides layers of earth and pebbles.

Local folklore insisted that it covered the tomb of a mythical ruler called King Zel (pronounced 'Sil' in the Wiltshire dialect). The name 'Silbury' was probably the only basis for this tradition. King Zel's corpse within the mound was believed to be clad in golden armour and mounted on his favourite horse, slaughtered for the purpose. In this manner, Zel was said to haunt Silbury Hill, riding round the monument on his horse, his armour gleaming in the moonlight. This is folklore, but in more recent years another apparition has been seen at Silbury: a headless figure standing on the summit.

Just a few of the prehistoric standing stones at Avebury, with the haunted Red Lion pub in the background. iStock

There is no tradition to explain this phantom but one can't help pondering the fact that the ancient Celts liked to collect skulls from beheaded victims: perhaps this ghost recalls some barbaric ritual of the distant past.

While Silbury Hill overlooks the Avebury circles, it in turn is overlooked by another prehistoric mound, this time one which definitely did contain burials. The West Kennet Long Barrow consists of several stone chambers covered by an earthen mound more than 300 feet (100 metres) long. The chambers contained the incomplete skeletons of more than forty people. The barrow is supposedly visited on the longest day of the year by the ghostly figure of a man described as 'a priest' who is accompanied by a large white hound with red ears. Both priest and dog enter the burial chambers but do not emerge again. The longest day of the year, or Summer Solstice, is an important date in the calendar of pre-Christian religions and dogs answering to the above description appear frequently in fairy traditions, suggesting they may be recollections of some ancient breed. These factors and the nature of the place being haunted suggest that these 'ghosts' may represent folk memories of some long-forgotten ritual.

Intriguingly, a similar white hound is also said to haunt the remains of another prehistoric tomb, the so-called Devil's Den at Fyfield Down, near Marlborough. This animal is said to have blazing red eyes. Near Stonehenge, on Salisbury Plain, is a burial mound called Doghill Barrow, which was said to get its name from a ghostly dog seen on its summit. No description of this hound has come down to modern times, unfortunately. Hundreds of prehistoric burial mounds can be found in Wiltshire, although none are as grand as West Kennet. Several of them have ghost stories attached to them. Travellers walking by night over Roundway Down would sometimes see someone ahead of them on the path. Many followed the shadowy figure, assuming it was someone who knew the way over the hill. But instead it would lead them to an old barrow, into which it would then vanish.

The sound of galloping hoof beats have been heard in the vicinity of Adam's Grave, a prominent mound on the summit of Walker's Hill. No horse is seen but it sounds like an entire army is thundering past. Gun's Church is an odd name given to a barrow near the village of Hill Deverill. It too is haunted by the sound of hoof beats and sometimes the rattling of chains. The ghost of keen sportsman Henry Croker, lord of the local manor house who died in 1730, is said to follow his hounds in a gallop round Gun's Church and this is supposed to account for the sounds.

In the foreground, slabs of stone belonging to the West Kennet Long Barrow, with Silbury Hill in the middle distance. Both monuments are said to be haunted.
iStock

Kit's Grave is a tumulus standing near a crossroads at Vernditch. 'Kit' is a corruption of an Anglo-Saxon name but according to the local ghost story, Kit was in fact a young woman who had killed herself after an unhappy love affair. She took the drastic measure of throwing herself down a well in the nearby churchyard. Her sad spirit was said ever after to linger around Kit's Grave.

A stand of trees marks the location of two of Wiltshire's hundreds of prehistoric burial mounds. Several of the county's barrows are said to be haunted. iStock

An amusing story was recorded in the 19th century about Manton Barrow, near Marlborough. After the mound was excavated and the skeleton found inside had been taken away to a museum, an old woman who lived in a neighbouring cottage claimed she was being visited by the restless spirit of its former occupant. She complained to her doctor that 'every night since that man came and disturbed the old creature, she did come out of the mound and walk around the house and "squinny" into the window. I do hear her most nights and want you to give me summat to keep her away.'

She presumably thought that the doctor, being an educated man, would know how to see off a ghost. Instead, he simply gave his troubled patient a strong sleeping draught. Calling on her several days later, she told him: 'The old creature came round the cottage as usual for a few nights but, not seeing me, gave up, thinking, no doubt, she had scared me away.'

More ancient phantoms of the Wiltshire countryside can be met with in the concluding chapter.

GHOSTS IN THE OPEN AIR

Wiltshire is a largely rural county, with half of its wide and varied landscape designated as Areas of Outstanding Natural Beauty. A particularly prominent feature of the Wiltshire landscape is its downland, ranges of high, grassy chalk hills which fall away to the farming country below.

In her book *Haunted Wiltshire*, Sonia Smith tells an interesting tale of an unusual ghost encountered along the summit of Cherhill Down. The hill is significant for bearing both a Neolithic settlement, Oldbury Hill Fort, and one of Wiltshire's many white horses carved into its side. Across it runs a Roman road, now a tree-lined track. It was beside this track, according to the author's account, that a woman named Catherine Stanton decided to camp one warm summer's evening with her two dogs. After a meal and a few glasses of wine, Catherine dozed but was awoken at about midnight by her dogs growling. A little unnerved, Catherine calmed her dogs while peering anxiously into the darkness to see who or what might be about intrude upon her lonely campsite. Sonia Smith takes up the story:

'A coach and four was rattling along the track in the distance towards them, the horses' feet drumming at a canter, the driver urging them on with shouts and the crack of a whip. Catherine watched in amazement. Then, suddenly, from out of nowhere there appeared two other riders approaching the coach from the nearside. One went across its bows, bringing it to a sudden halt, making the horses rear. He held a gun towards the driver. The other pushed what looked like a pistol through the coach window. It was a hold-up. Three other riders also appeared, now surrounding the coach. As Catherine stared in disbelief at what she was seeing, she also realised that all the horsemen were completely naked! All wore tricorn hats but nothing else!'

This bizarre tableau continued for a minute longer, after which the naked highwaymen cantered off, firing a couple of triumphant pistol shots into the air, and the coachman geed up his horses to continue the journey. The coach began to rattle at some speed towards the startled Catherine, who grabbed her dogs and jumped out of its way. The phantom melted into nothingness moments later, however. Some years later, Catherine learned of an old Wiltshire folk tale reading a gang of highwaymen who used to rob coaches naked so that no one would recognise their faces. It was told as a joke, but Catherine had good reason to wonder whether the tall tale was true after all.

Other witnesses have related encounters with the shades of Roman soldiers still marching along this ancient track. An old shepherd who tended his flocks on Cherhill Down told Kathleen Wiltshire of 'a lot of men a'marchin' [and] they did wear skirts'. He seemed mildly offended by this, to him, peculiar dress sense. When Mrs Wiltshire asked him whether he was sure the figures were male, he confirmed: 'Oh, yes, they did have beards, some on 'em, and they wore girt helmets – wi' 'air across the top … and had a girt bird on a pole a'front on 'em.' The 'girt bird' was, of course, Rome's imperial eagle.

Another ghost of the Roman period, that of a centurion riding a horse, is said to haunt another prehistoric track, the Ridgeway, where it passes Market Lavington. Near Woodmanton, a valley called Patty's Bottom is believed to have been the scene of a fierce fight between Ancient Britons and invading Romans. After dark the sounds of the battle are said to still be heard and the gruesome spectres of headless horses

Cherhill Down, haunted by Roman soldiers and a gang of very unusual highwaymen. iStock

have been seen galloping on the hills above. Another possibly ancient apparition is that of a 'white-robed figure', resembling the common image of a Druid, which has been met with on Imber Down, near West Lavington.

The Wansdyke is a ditch and embankment raised in the Dark Ages as a defensive boundary marker. Its name is a contraction of 'Woden's Dyke', Woden being the chief god of the Anglo-Saxons. On a stretch of the Wansdyke in All Cannings parish, a phantom funeral procession has been seen. It consists of a group of men carrying torches in advance of a wagon carrying a coffin. The wagon is pulled by black horses and on the lid of the coffin there lies a crown or circle of gold. It may possibly be the apparition of the royal cortege of some obscure Saxon king or queen, but there are no records of such a procession. Katherine Wiltshire points out that a medieval retelling of the King Arthur story tells of Sir Lancelot leading a torch-lit procession taking Queen Guinevere's body from Amesbury to Glastonbury Abbey, and she wonders whether this is the route they took.

Mrs Wiltshire was also able to shed light on another apparition seen on the Wansdyke. On the stretch which passes over Tan Hill, near Allington, a young girl experienced a most unusual twist on the haunted house theme, for in this case the house *was* the ghost. From the hill she clearly saw a house which apparently didn't exist. She was able to describe it in detail, including the stable block from which she could see a horse's head peering out, but not even the oldest resident could recall a house ever having stood where she saw it. This was in the 1960s. Some years later, Mrs Wiltshire happened to be looking through some old illustrations of the county and found one showing a house, much as described, in the place where the

The Wansdyke at Morgan's Hill. A spectral funeral cortege has been met with along this ancient earthwork. iStock

girl had seen it. The property had been demolished a long time before.

A beautiful but ghostly girl dressed all in white strolls along the road skirting the foot of Tan Hill. A travelling preacher who encountered her in 1904 described his astonishment at seeing the girl during a heavy downpour, apparently unaffected by the rain. His horse had stopped dead in its tracks at the sight of the girl, and it dawned on the preacher that there was something unearthly about her. He vividly recalled her 'angelic' face framed by a mass of auburn hair. As she drew level with him, she vanished.

On the road below Morgan's Hill, near Calne, a nightbound traveller encountered a phantom funeral procession that may well have been the same as that seen at All Cannings, for the Wansdyke continues on its way close by. The witness took off his cap as it passed towards the turning for Blackland, believing it to be a real cortege, but then it suddenly melted away before his eyes. A similar spectre has been seen on the outskirts of Sandfield, near Potterne.

Near the tiny village of Bowerchalke can be found a wide depression in the ground forming a natural amphitheatre. The feature goes by the unglamorous name of Pug's Hole. Tradition states that many moons ago an old shepherd became caught in a blizzard and stumbled into Pug's Hole, where he became trapped in a deep snowdrift. As he struggled to get back out again, the numbing cold slowly paralysing him, he cried repeatedly, but more and more faintly, for help; help which never came. His pitiful cries are said to still be heard emanating from Pug's Hole on winter nights.

Durnford Down is haunted by an invisible horse. It has been heard galloping across the hill near Red House Farm. Although it cannot be seen, those who have heard it believe that 'someone' must be riding it, for the creaking of a leather saddle can be detected. Sheep have been known to scatter in terror as the ghost gallops past.

Phantom horses and horsemen are also encountered on Wiltshire's highways and byways. A headless horseman patrols a path called Sloan's Track, near Stourton. His story is a grim one. He made a bet that he could ride his horse from Wincanton Market back to Stourton in just seven minutes. The attempt was too much for his horse, however, and it stumbled along Sloan's Track, throwing its reckless rider to the ground with such impact that he broke his neck. The ghost being headless suggests that this story is incomplete, for folk tales recorded elsewhere relate that similarly foolish wagers ended with the rider hitting the low branch of a tree, resulting in the head being severed from the body.

The ghost of the notorious highwayman William Boulter, best known for haunting Marlborough (see the 'Ghosts About Town' chapter), is said to also gallop down a stretch of the A30 and to be seen on the roads criss-crossing Salisbury Plain. Further phantom horsemen have been spotted along the A365 near Atworth.

The apparition haunting Savernake Forest is of a horsewoman rather than a man. England's only privately owned forest (it closes to the public one day a year to restore that unique status), Savernake has been in the hands of the Seymour family for centuries. The identity of the ghostly woman who

A headless woman on horseback has been seen riding through Savernake Forest. iStock

rides among the stately trees is a mystery, for she is missing her head.

Savernake Forest is not the only haunted wood in Wiltshire. Sally in the Woods, a rather lonely area of trees and scrubs on the Somerset border, has a decidedly eerie reputation. In his *Paranormal Wiltshire*, David Scanlan tells of motorists driving through Sally in the Woods and being accosted by 'disembodied voices, the sounds of a baby crying [and] terrifying screams', as well as having glimpses of the apparition of a small boy. The more commonly seen ghost is that of a woman, thought to have been a Gypsy who was imprisoned and starved to death in a Victorian folly tower which overlooks the area. She has been seen crossing the road and there are rumours that drivers have even given her lifts!

A phantom plane was seen to crash into woodland near Larkhill, a military base near Stonehenge. Larkhill has the distinction of having been the first military aerodrome in Britain. Sir Michael Bruce was one of those who witnessed the apparition. Bruce served in both World Wars and later became an African explorer and a travel writer, as well as a glider instructor (he was also the elder brother of Nigel Bruce, the actor famous for playing a bumbling Dr Watson opposite Basil Rathbone's Sherlock Holmes). On 23 December 1953, Sir Michael recalled the incident, which had taken place during World War II, in a letter to the *Evening Standard* newspaper. He wrote:

'Shortly before D-Day [i.e. 6 June 1944], I was sent on a course of instruction to Larkhill. Four of us went with an RAF W/O in a jeep to select suitable gunsites; we were coming up from the north towards the road which runs past Stonehenge, and between us and the road lay a small copse; suddenly we all saw a very small aircraft dive straight down into the wood and disappear in the trees; we raced the jeep up to give assistance; there was no sign of a crash – nothing – nothing flying away to the south.

'Suddenly I heard the W/O shout; he was standing white-faced before a large stone cairn commemorating the first death from an aeroplane accident in this country in 1912. It has been suggested that the apparition was that of Colonel F.S. [*sic.*] Cody, pioneer of military aviation, who died nearby in his experimental aircraft. His was actually the first death in powered heavier-than-air flight; but the monument refers to Captain B. Loraine and S/Sergeant R. Wilson, who died in

The wreckage of Colonel Cody's ill-fated 'Floatplane' in which he and one other man died. Sir Michael Bruce believed that this was the aircraft he and others saw as a nose-diving phantom on Salisbury Plain.

1912, the first members of the RFC [Royal Flying Corps] to do so.'

Colonel Cody (his initials were actually S.F. for Samuel Franklin) was an extraordinary character. An American, born in Iowa, his real surname was Cowdery but he changed his surname in tribute to his hero, 'Buffalo Bill' Cody. Like Buffalo Bill, S.F. Cody became a cowboy entertainer running his own Wild West show, but he was more than just a showman. Cody developed the War-Kites which were used during World War I as a smaller and more efficient alternative to barrage balloons. Having settled in England, he developed a motorised kite which, in 1907, became in effect Britain's first aeroplane and Cody was, of course, its first pilot. His fatal crash occurred while testing a new design of aeroplane, which he had called the Cody Floatplane. His passenger, a cricketer named William Evans, also died in the crash.

Also related to transport are the ghostly phenomena related to the Box Tunnel, near the village of Box in the west of the county. The railway tunnel is two miles (3km) long and is of some considerable age, for it was built by none other than Isambard Kingdom Brunel. It is said that on Brunel's birthday, 9 April, the sun shines straight through the tunnel. For many years a ghost train – of the supernatural rather than the fairground variety – was reported to be seen hurtling through Box Tunnel. Great Western Railway men working within it claim to have been startled by the sudden appearance of the ghostly locomotive rushing past them. It was so dark in the tunnel and so clogged with soot that it was supposedly impossible even to see the lighted carriage windows of a normal train as it passed, and yet the phantom train was clear as day.

In their book *Shadows in the Steam: The Haunted Railways of Britain*, David Brandon and Alan Brooke relate further phenomena from the Box Tunnel. According to the authors, more than a hundred men lost their lives during its construction. Shadowy figures have been seen by engine drivers silhouetted against the light of the tunnel's mouth. Others working on the track claim to have seen more distinct apparitions dressed in the fashions of their 19th-century forebears. Over the years the ghost train itself seems to have faded to a sound only, of hissing steam and rushing metal, bursting from the exit.

Finally, we must consider the Black Dogs which legend has it patrol the Wiltshire countryside. These are traditional spooks reported in the folklore of almost every county in the UK. Generally they are described, as the name would suggest, as huge hounds with black coats. Sometimes they have enormous, glaring eyes. They tend to wander ancient tracks and lonely lanes, literally dogging the footsteps of travellers after dark. Kathleen Wiltshire collected many encounters in the county with these monstrous mutts.

One of them was to be met with on the edge of Savernake Forest at Deane Water Bottom – 'a very lonely spot,' according to Mrs Wiltshire. Rumour had it the Black Dog was the spirit of a murderer of long ago but others simply referred to it as 'the Devil'. A 'shaggy dog' had a habit of scaring the work-horses at a farm at Hinton Brook, and another terrified a Women's Institute member as she was taking a walk down Abingdon Court Lane in Cricklade. A Black Dog 'wi' eyes as big as saucers' would be seen sitting on a 'stone-heap' (an ancient cairn perhaps?) by the roadside at Coate, home village of the celebrated writer on country matters, Richard Jefferies.

A real train emerges from the two-mile long tunnel at Box Hill, where ghostly locos and long-dead railway workers have also been seen. iStock

The spectral hound haunting a road near Crockerton was especially alarming. It had 'bristling hair' and was capable of 'blowing fire from its nostrils'!

Finally, near Chapmanslade there are a number of places named after the Black Dogs haunting them. The hound haunting Black Dog Farm was supposed to have belonged to one of two men who fell in love with the same girl. When they fought a duel, the dog attacked and killed the rival suitor. The tale connected to a similar ghost at nearby Black Dog Hill stated that it had been owned by a highwayman who trained it to jump on the coachman before he held up a coach. Also in the neighbourhood is a Black Dog Wood. The stretch of the A36 which passes by the wood is haunted by a hound with blazing eyes. It was considered an omen of death: anyone unlucky enough to see it 'would be dead by Christmas'.

Sherlock Holmes and Dr Watson catch sight of The Hound of the Baskervilles in Conan Doyle's famous story. This fictional hound was inspired by legends of spectral black dogs such as those encountered in Wiltshire